Original cover art concept, design, direction, and idea by:
Gissel Grizzle

Drawn and digitally illustrated by: Elias Curtis of
Transformed Designs

Dedication

To every soul who has ever felt hopeless and inadequate remember that expression of your authentic self will help you to unveil love for your true self. Be you unapologetically.

Track List

Intro

The Purpose

Riddle me this who takes your money and leaves doses of
hope to the unsound mind delivering love to the unkind
Enchanted goddess turning words into lines
Who is she?
The Poetic Messiah

Untitled Dedication

I would have let you stand on my shoulders to get to Zion
I would have given you my heart to feel the love I still
have inside for you
I would have taken out my teeth so you could smile
I would have died to give you more time
I would have given you my mind to make memories just
to see you and make myself me again
I would have tried to conquer my fears
I would have been more prepared
I would have given you my eyes to see the beauty inside
the ugliest sight
I would have given you my hands to feel the fibers of life
I would have given you my lips to ask for another chance

Dark Child

Black skin
Black hair
Black womb
Black thought
Is she
There are complexities in her complexion
Non-conforming attitude most mistake for being rude
She was often misunderstood
The little girl inside her always possessed dark attributes
Some mistook her for the devil
Back then she
Just wanted to be loved for who she was
She was a Goddess
Suppressing her powers to create and transform
Her mission
To sit still in darkness
Upon coming of age she would conspire with her womb
To fabricate
children who ran wild
who thought free
who harnessed light

Messiah

The alchemist in me was never polite
Leading sheep with my vision whilst I remained out of
sight
Fright was written on their faces
One by one I left bread crumbs and shone light inside the
unknown
Come with me I beckoned
Still they opted to stay home

The Gift

You've repeated the same things
It lacks rhythm
It's obvious that misery loves you
One can tell by the way you've always complained that it's
raining when your garden is in full bloom
Neighbor's planters pot fascinates you
Continue to look over there
Marvel the square footage of beauty
While you sit on acres

Weekend in the Lion's Den

I'm writing this letter to inform
you that the misfits came while you were gone
They were scantily clad
And black lips they donned with rouge
I tried to tell them that you
did not fancy their kind
but they laughed and pushed me to the side

Lady Dandelion

Institutionalized by eyes that are trapped inside grey
matter
The margins become narrow every time I walk outside
I'm no flower
I'm a weed who grows despite a gardener's efforts
Green and fertile
At times stubborn yellow
A gardener's dream is to have a manicured lawn free of
flaws
You see what they don't know is why I frequent their yard.

Goddess

Cleaning vomit stains from the carpet
Drunk from the times I forgot to love myself
I remember when I waited for them
To caress my flesh and tell me it
Was worthy
But the repugnant smell of my high
esteem repelled them

Amplitude

Lost one

Stopped writing for a while
The well of thought dried up
Wind elevated the feathers out of reach
Lost all six senses on a train to nowhere fast
Fear paralyzed everything real
No distinguished characters
Silenced chatter
A dusty desk paper cluttered
Nothingness finally mattered
The worst came in the final days of November

Third Eye

She has been so removed
She has no desire to interact
Actions of malice breathes
but her soul is still intact
Nothing bothers her anymore
Her eyes are filled with openness
Peek inside dirty mildewed mirrors
You aren't welcome here
Say hello
compliment her
But don't anticipate a reaction
Stand still
Delve deeper into her silence
Don't grieve her sadness
She smiled at her reflection

Self

And they came but there was nothing here. No doors, no windows on the house, but there was silence. Forgiveness lied in the dark narrow passage while fear lingered on the left side.

Gathering the ruffles of courage, she kissed her reflection. She put on white satin that quickly turned brown with her essence and she was sure she was ready for marriage. She held on to the little girl inside herself and vowed to keep her safe.

The Day I Woke Up

No fairytale it seems the end is near and many are
scrambling with fear. Relaxed, I twirled wooly coils
around my fingers as I began to count backwards. A black
veil covered commitments to the darkest parts. Light
beams caused me to squint at everyone around me. I was
apprehensive behind my calm demeanor. At war with
everything they ever taught me about myself. Feuding
with those who I once considered allies. Standing behind
enemy lines and cross fires, I walked bare feet onto middle
grounds.
I was ready to die.

Rebirth

Thought absorbs into being.
Carefully she selected who she wanted to be.
Hastily halting human doing and morphed into being.

Lioness

There's knowledge and wisdom that emanates
from my bones
Years of history that has never been told
I command with spells of silence

Conflicted

Nightly conversations with the moon I asked
Is the sky really blue?
Everything you left inside of me is acid
Volcanic ashes that seeped into the ocean
Formed islands around us
Mounds of quick sand
I stuck my feet in foolishly
You captured my mind and I sank
palm trees bended my intuition
I loved it
Because I hadn't known better

Sixty-Nine

My flesh wanted a new beginning something like pearl,
something like diamonds, my spirit was already satisfied
with living. Perhaps my soul likes the thrill of
transforming into trees, rivers, and mountains.

Song

Loose worn strings barely clung to wooden skin
The wand stroked my hairs like a violin
Beautiful cries filled the room
Once again
No one is listening

Maps of Peace

Maybe if I hung myself on the fragments of insults they
would be satisfied
Maybe if pieces of me disappeared after every attempt to
break me
their lives would be filled with richness in my absence
My mind has blueprints of escape routes to every country
In my dreams I've made peace with the pieces of me that
were not valued by them
and I've created new continents to expand my love of self

The Evolution of me

Pulling myself by my belly across the land
No idea where I'm going
No feet to stand
Crawling
Crouched down with a vision in my two hands
Seeking out my feet to stand
Discovered the warmth of my mother's hand and
stumbled down the belly of the unknown
Drowning with arms flailing I called out to my father
He pulled me out to safety and fed me to chaos
Peace was a distant relative
Until I was courted by the sun

She

Sway in her hips
Arch in her back
Her womb is soil
She buds in the face of patriarchy

Reign

I think I thought I would I shouldn't have
But I did
In the end all I could do was laugh because I had gotten
frustrated with
The way the word victim framed my being
Enough I said
And became free

Exile

Producing soulful lines from the "cubbyhole"
They often banished me to
Confined they thought
Meanwhile I practiced my signature
Writing it in blood so they knew it was permanent

Fear

I presume you'd like to enter here by the way you're
always inquiring
There were many others who attempted
to calculate the distance between terror and light
It's further from being understood closer to being felt and
blinding

Dusty Foot Burglar

Tears hit the pavement like thunderstorms
As the sun dried it I laughed to myself
Wondering how I let con-artists kidnap my happiness

Anti-Social

Too much laugh out loud
Not enough quite reflection
I said a few words maybe a bit under
140 characters
I had no filter
60 seconds of raw presence
Still not enough to capture their
Attention

Cotton

Passion turned cold
The flame
Blue hydrogen
Red oxygen
Molecules floated
Iron
Copper
Brass
Two sides of a golden coin
She's an impoverished soul who took her wealth back

Sound Bite

People can only see the photo that you've painted, but beyond analyzing and interpretation it says so much more than what they are allowed to see despite them experiencing it themselves.

Love is an exuberant battlefield it continues to wound 7 billion people and counting daily. Nothing will stop this warfare not even a diplomatic verbal exchange between leaders.

I've found beauty in the blisters and ash of a mother's feet, one who has walked miles to find her youth something to eat. That's true beauty skin without scars are papers waiting to be written on.

Nothing is worse than dying miserable. Without leaving your signature in the universe. Don't be too scared of how your penmanship looks. Leave your mark any way.

The job that brings me wealth is not a 9 to 5 it is self-work.

The Beat

Muddy Lane

The cup-board, the doors, the floors store pieces of me at
4415
Dreams of a better home packed up and moved across the
state line
Hoped that things would get better over time
Nothing changed
Christmas sorrows are much colder now
And the memories though distant still come to visit every
holiday
Some even come to stay
The weight of being filled with lies and illusions of family
breaks the chair
No one hears me falling
No one hears the thud
They all continue smiling and passing the salad and the
carrot juice to their right
My mind yearns to take flight
The best way out he said
Through the window of a three story brick house

Broken Bonds

I ain't gon' front and say I'm happy and all smiles. It's shit
so fucking tormenting that leaves me hollow inside. These
eyes bright and brown, but my soul is tired.
Tired of trying. Fake ass people say they got you, but you
know they lying. Where were you when I was crying. You
parasites rich from mining my mind. If these words make
you feel a way, it's probably you I'm talking about. They
say the truth will set you free so it's time it came out.

Suicide Hotline

Hold on, shh no miss I'm here to help you.
No! No! No!
You will never understand, she said touching my hand.
Bruised lip and chin sore from the night before. Are you
sure?
I asked. I could tell she was numb.
Tired, spit, chewed, melancholy and dirty like the gum on
the bottom of their shoes.

Open letter

Thank you for years of silence
Many came to help
Your lips were sealed and my soul was barren
For twenty-five years I tried to conceive
Nothing was born
Every night I laid with sorrow
And kissed sheets of anxiety goodnight
Shame raped me and fearful offspring ran
around my house whispering
That I was cursed

Dwellings

If I pissed in a solo cup and called it lemonade would you
drink it?
Well I've had to pretend like the life time supply of rotten
limes you've brought to me was an ice cold beverage
To make living with you more digestible

Bitch

To you I'm less than the diluted cup of red wine that sits
on the living room table
Only thing we shared is the oven of which we both came
from
To utter the words "my brother" feels like death on my
tongue,
like poison to my breath, like being gassed and lit to burn
alive, like being hung upside down inside a butcher's
sanctuary
I can't drink and eat with you
My gut is filled with fear, but on your plate my self-worth
is being shredded by the knife and fork you've had a tight
grasp of for a while
Are you not full from dining on my power to fight back?
Or have you saved the rest for the potbellied pig who
trampled your feet and knocked over the goose who lays
the golden eggs?

The Interview

Father why are you drinking so much?
What are you trying to cover up?
Is it hidden?
Have you found it in the bottom of that cup?

Weekly Entertainment

I've scrubbed till my palms were bare
Like raw meat
Cleaning up the mess you made
All the crevices are filled with dusty hope
No sweeping
No dusting
Will ever keep this house clean
Constantly spot treating our unresolved issues
There are massive humps under the carpets
I hope the visitors don't trip when they come over
To the summer BBQ's
And On Christmas
And Thanksgiving

Interlude

Verse 1

It's unfortunate that I never got to see you smile again
Laughter that bellowed through quite rooms have become
distant whispers
A touch becomes a memory
A kiss leaves traces of your spirit behind
I won't say this is my loss but rather I am lost because I
can't find my way back to your warm hugs and our
conversations
I'm confused not sure if I want to see you on life support
I just want to remember you sitting upright and sipping on
my homemade fruit smoothie
The world should know about your warmth
It's the kind that babies dream of
That family and friends find comfort
But when you are not physically here it is the warmth that
fills the space in our hearts after you're gone

Verse 2

Venom penetrates and I am no victim
There will be no need for an ambulance please don't call
911 I need to feel this
I am sweating and surges of electricity follows narrowed
paths and blackens my veins
Delirium hits but I never had pain as sweet as this.
I am convinced that the rattle sounds like Africa
welcoming me back.
In a pit of serpents, I lie in the nude, a python's embrace is
where I discovered solitude
The illicit being who will not scream when swallowed
We are one soul that surpasses growing old
There is no time just space to be occupied and together we
are gypsies

Verse 3

They vowed to keep the silence
But thoughts spoke volumes in their children's face
Though some were identical how could orchids bloom in
cement?
Sailed away hopes like tampons in waste baskets
We've adopted them
We love the strange things
Compiled all the weird ones
And placed them on their backs to air dry in no specific
height
Creed or genes in the mid-day summer breeze

Verse 4

When I am with you love songs are equivalent to the
peaceful symphony of a waterfall
in your absence love songs are the stains from tears that
form crystals on my brown cheek
The ocean of misery that drowns me each night
but I manage to rise above deep waters and stand on the
sand
Until I see the shadows of your face and I dive in again
I've died a sweet death
In my last breath I managed to kiss the ripples which held
a still image of the dimples I nick named Gissel's Cavern
Yes
Paradise at last is this what God's look like?

Verse 5

Bring me a man who can dance with my soul and sit out
on the porch afternoon after afternoon till we are pruned
Give me a glass of passion so we can toast to years of
excellence
Fetch me some more time to reminisce and quench my
thirst with liquid memories
I am not alive, tell him to breath into me and tell them to
name her life

Verse 6

I've been here before
This place in the middle of nowhere, but it still exists
A place where I can truly be myself,
but it seems so unfamiliar to me like
I never been here before
Everything seems out of place like my shit has been
tampered with
but everything is where I left it.
A state of confusion, a house of anxiety, a country of
sorrow
I've got no money, no prospective place to move
but damn I just got to get out of here
out of my comfort zone

Verse 7

Black daises in my garden
Cherry wine fills my senses
I'm standing still and the wind blows through my essence
I reach down and touch my shadow to ensure that it's still
intact
Stand upright once more with my back to the sun
Reminiscing on the nights when I was a child
The expeditions I had in the Forrest
Now the trees are no longer there
The smog is thickened and I can't breathe
there isn't a glimpse of air
Somehow I believe it's safer to stay here

Verse 8

I'm not perfect and only a God can judge me
I'm not a saint but she is loyalty
When I feel less than beautiful she accepts it
she knows I am moody at times yet she holds my hands
without regret
She is unconditional love
I feel at ease to know
She sees beneath the external wall that I've hid under
I am liberated from soul snatchers
Continuing to live and enjoy my happily ever after
Because I was told that death is the beginning of a new
chapter

Verse 9

Excuse me while I build on this for a little
The debris jolted in the middle and abruptly stopped there
So high up I saw my dreams in the star's faces
Quickly it's all snatched from me and I'm on the ground
I should have no problems with the soil that grows
everything I need right?
I love you Mother Nature you've nourished this soul
Till it has outgrown me and I'm spilling over won't you
have a sip of my love, my love?
I want to be the line that widens frown lines into a smile,
the one who turns tears into fountains that will grant your
every wish
The summer breeze that cools your quick temper
And the plant that cures all your ailments
I'm sorry I'm still building I'm working with an overgrown
soul so it takes me a while longer

Verse 10

I spoke into the ears of the wind about my hopes that I will
see you again
She brought my message to the sky and tears cascaded
down onto our soil
Weeks have passed, vines are fully grown to the highest
peaks of the mountains,
The grapes are sweet and fermented wine
Years have passed and we gaze into frozen time
We perspire
Droplets trickle off our bodies turn into wine
I am instantly reminded why when I close my eyes
Time rocks me forward on its pendulum
Deeper and deeper I go inside

Verse 11

Go to school, get a job, retire in 40 years
Be an outstanding citizen
Suppress those tears
Don't live life, fear will keep you safe
Don't speak up,
Look down when spoken to
Never open the vault where dreams are lined in gold
Nothing good ever came from the unknown
Laugh, but not too loud they will hear you
Give, but not too much
Don't love
Hearts too warm
Too much room for a revolution
Misery fuels the cars on the 95
And the MTA engines are the only thing alive

Verse 12

Have I lived trying to be alive?
All I feel are my inadequacies
Being happy is a mere fantasy
I cry and the world rotates as per usual
I walk and the concrete feels like air underneath
Any attempts to sing becomes stifled by the involuntary
silence
In a room the velvet couch leaves no remnants of my ass
when I get up
I write and the pen leaves no trace
Words in mass incarceration
A long sentence to being the invisible woman

Verse 13

The fear came by late last night and sat by my bedside
It tried to convince me that all is well
despite me not being able to move a muscle
Stroking my face as it persuaded me to close my eyes
Cold sweat drenched the cot
I laid still
Terror cuddled the will to stay awoke
Tripped and stumbled into the realm of darkness
Disoriented I walked into a nightmare
He was there and his eyes glared with intimidation

Bass

Levels to Understanding

I wanted him to fuck me
Raw
Deep
Drip
And uncensored
Open my mind fondle my thoughts
Come with me
Don't start no shit that can't be finished
Leaving me on the edge
Stroking cerebral wetness
Sending me into an asylum
Don't pull out I begged
His head swelled
I'm elevated

Body Count

I'm a sin disguised as someone else
The many men I've slept with I can't imagine how much
I've degraded myself
Love, or lust, or infatuation made me do it,
Was it the dick, the lips, the way he stroked me while
holding my hips I'm a sin
Now I'm struggling to be someone's significant other
If he only knew how many knocked on my door, he would
leave me for sure, I am sin
Should I ever get married in the near future my groom
should spit at my face instead of caressing it with a soft
kiss.
My gown should be the color of dirt as a reminder of what
I'm truly worth.
Hell isn't good enough for me and although I have faith
even the lord will hesitate to let me enter near heaven's
gate.
I'm a sin

Muse

I fell in love with an artist once
Lustful gazes and acrylic painted kisses
He was my easel
I was his canvas
And together we fabricated on different mediums
Graffiti garnished back alleys
art shows and galleries.

Lust

As I turned around to walk away he said, "I'm checking
you out,"
I smiled
Already checked out
Not searching for the love bragged about on mcm
Looking at his eyes to see a tender reflection of myself,
But all I saw were my legs spread and my body laid flat on
the edge of his bed

Relations

There were words
None on the cusp to portray action
Just promises that her heart used to flutter for
tracing her footsteps
Nothing of substance, nothing concrete
Just air to walk on
At this point she stepped out of chalk line dreams
to pursue reality

Standards

Woke up to an unfamiliar scent that hurled my
subconscious into a frenzy. I knew something wasn't right,
who the fuck was that stranger arousing me last night? It's
noon and I still smell like him. Parts of me find comfort in
familiarity, yet I'm still not accustomed.
Still sure I deserve more.
I know I won't acknowledge old romance
wrapped in maroon blankets.
I guess it's nothing to understand.
Everything above and below me has standards.
Ain't like I couldn't have him
It was too easy
a King would be a
challenge.

Verses to my Love

Watching a bulb pierce through cement is a phenomenon
But while they all stood and gazed you saw me coming
beyond galaxies
Soft petals rose from callused roots
You watered even on days where no cracks showed visible
signs of earth
You held your head down to whisper beauty into shadows
of despair
Placed signs around me to indicate there is someone
growing inside there
Most days I couldn't hear
My roots ached
The concrete teared
Tear filled chlorophyll
Spilled out onto the streets and vines ran down the lines of
boulevards and backyards and backward
toward muddy skin
Two starry moons shone onto petals that lay on the
ground of our garden on Kossuth street

Falsetto

Black Almond

I cried
Listening to Donell Jones
Discovered that's where I want to be
Duets with Lauryn singing,
No one loves you more than me
Hurts so bad to listen to the same old song on a Weeknd
Numb sitting in Linkin Park
I'm always here won't you dance with me
Why don't I just let go Neyo is on the phone
I choose you won't you stay
No you won't, No you won't
because you're still the one that got away

Memory Ville

Salt around lips
Margaritas in bloodstreams
Arms around waist
Drawn closer till there is no more space
Sip slow, savor the sweet sensual sounds by the sea
Hurry before winter freezes the sand it can be slippery
Remember our spot

Notes in a furnace

The butterflies
No longer fluttering gracefully
Haste to break free from the depths of a heavy womb
Used to tickle me flushed pink
Used to be sunshine and crescent moons
Memories that smiled fought through gloom
Wet,
sticky,
bittersweet,
ashy crusted,
molded wings
Evolved into swarms of wondering bees
Won't you please leave me alone

Frequency

Time hasn't healed anything
Pendulums don't exist
Clocks don't tick tock
Digital time doesn't illuminate the dark shadows in my
room
Passports don't exist
Visited many places without the wings of a plane
All is there
Dug an arm through dimensions
Stood still in vibrations
Other worlds exist outside of the 3D perception

Paradise Island

I had a dream that you stopped by and dropped of a gift
Attached was a card which inscribed your name in faded
letters that read H-r-r-s-n
Boxes filled with candied goodies, lots of red
Valentine's Day had fell on December 25th
I wrote you a card too...Hmm Hmm
It sits on my desk under a stack of books as I compose the
infinite series
The slice of cheesecake I offered is on the second
compartment in my fridge
The invitation of an embrace and a kiss on the cheek
awaits a rsvp
The heart still persists and the mind stages holographs of a
reunion

So what

Writing every day
Some to say to say
Hey!
How is your day?
Insults via text?
I miss you
Can we see each other?
Embrace.
K-i-s-s-i-n-g.
So many words so many spells
Light and dark dancing why should love stay still
Not a single witch on a broom they all have someone
Boiling cauldron says
"Too bad he's with me"
I tipped it over and watched green goop flood floors
A mess that no janitor would clean
But I would
Harsh words pierced me several times
That night I was up till sunrise
Body quivering, heart racing
Doing meditation and dancing to tribal music brought me
gifts of a peaceful slumber the following night

Paper Weights

Do you still have the letters and the photo I gave to you?
The ones placed over you like halos in heaven
I am not dead
My spirit is still alive in the breaths that crept inside you
once we locked lips
Still alive in the walls where you once laid your head
I haven't disappeared
There are no faces in obituaries
None on milk cartons or news channels
I'm still here
You can't get rid of my energy it can't be altered or
destroyed
More powerful than world famous magicians, and
celebrities,
You know not my name
I am
This is not an introduction I exist in you no need for
definition
Validation
Need no permission to caress that flesh
Water colored ink is left on your lips
An imprint from a soul like mine

Lovers stroll

Just don't say you never loved me I was a joke all along
That the nights we spent merging masculine and feminine
energies never existed
Just don't say to shut the fuck up
Like the night I sat on you in the driver's seat sucking your
lips and raising the hairs on both our bodies is a different
tongue that you never understood
Just don't tell me to stop loving you
You called me at night and told me you loved me
Remember
Just don't tell me I'm nothing
Hold me and say I was the best woman you ever met
Again
Howl at the red moon we saw when we wrote our names
in the sand
Just don't tell me you were unfaithful
I never held you against your will
Don't tell your new lover to bash me, like I didn't abort the
first seed
Just don't refuse to see me
In a mental institute I laid when there were no voices
inside my head
Don't cry as I poisoned self
Begging to numb my existence as the
life we created disappeared on a Maxi Pad
Just don't tell me to move on, you moved into your ex

Coldest Knight

No one told me
No one told me
But someone told me that he loved me
Said he'd be there when I got back
When I returned there were shadows in my spot
Unfamiliar and covered in shiny Armor
Saw my reflection and tried to say some words
Opened up the visor, darkness seeped out
I closed my eyes and took a step forward
This wasn't my lord he's never coming back as my love
In another dimension he is noble
King he is and Queen I am
Rulers of the motherland
Our children are masters of the universe
But no one told me, no one told me

Crescendo

After it happened

I was so ashamed, I went to the baby shower and I felt
everyone's eyes pierce my belly
Alright everyone
The music stopped everyone gathered
A few even drew closer and captured it with their camera
Chatter,
Laughter,
Smiles,
Boxes filled with petite pink clothes
A celebration inside a Brooklyn home
On the outside I was
Standing with guilt filled balloons
A mourning doorman
Running to the bathroom a dozen times to
wipe clear confetti out of my eyes
It was a celebration and all my family travelled from
yonder to witness an unsold product of love
I wonder if they knew you weren't in there anymore
Could they see how broken I was
Their relative no longer dwelled in my tiny cottage
I couldn't bare the subtle hints of he or she's blood in
the air. Murder. The only word in the dictionary located
walking distance to mother
They wouldn't be allowed inside anyways
The name Jessica was written on the door of the pediatric
unit.

Internal Suicide

Its 01.22.2009 02:38 pm
I'm running
I'm running
I'm running
Pause suddenly I'm thinking about jumping
So steep can't stop the adrenaline from rushing
Feels like the push I've been waiting for
I'm sinking
I'm sinking
I'm sinking
You might make it in time
Emotions scattered
The pain is unbearable
Bleeding uncontrollable
Holding the rope and knife
Standing at the bridge
Wondering how I'll end this misery

Cont'd

What do I do when life is not worth fighting for?
Is death more pleasant after all?
Have I thought about how my actions
will affect my loved ones?
Tragedy shatters their lives
Like broken glasses on street corners
Desperately needing to remove the splinters
If life is worth living
Role playing death is the only way I'll get my Oscar
A few standing ovations
Who will read the next script?
Who told you its better if I shall stay?
Zero dreams, hopes, aspirations beyond today
When the sun sets and night is born
Reminisce I'll be gone
For the fear of being unhappy after life appears
Physical flesh remains tear stained
Bloody roses snot filled noses vanish
The ink dries and I open my eyes
A Letter to my internal suicide

For my little brown girl

Daddy doesn't know how wonderful you are
He came here last night and took the car
He thinks you're too young to understand what's going on
Dinner for three are now a dinner for two
Unfinished bed time stories
Mommy lives down south and dad lives up north
The phone rings and she extends her hand and says it's for
you
Mommy sniffles, but doesn't have the flu
She's blue
She once was a little brown girl like you
Broken view from a black Nissan year 1992
Left with a will to drive
No time to stop and ask for directions
Long open roads
A hearse carried memories of a sacred union
Somehow all that is lost
Now she isn't welcome here
Like a piece of lint on the elite's jacket

Vision Board

Post cards from my backyard in Barbados
Looking down at sand the color of 5 years ago
I dunno how I ended up here
The sea was different colors of blue unbruised and salty
I was nude and I didn't give a fuck
I couldn't apologize for the way the sun wrapped its arms
around me because I was golden
My son was trees and he loved when father earth tossed
him on his shoulders and gave him piggy rides around our
beach house property
He giggled so loud

Sister Girl

You used to be so strong what happened to you
Your soul has become limber your bones have too
Sister girl no longer laughs at whimsical memories
She sits at the fire place crouched as tears fell into the
flames
They came to save Sister girl--
to find her already dead

Land of the Free

I'm having an identity crisis
I'm in the land of the lost but never found
Will anyone seek me out?
Tucked deep below the cracked sidewalks pain and
sorrow breaks legs, but also leads us to the most
spectacular places
It's the road to the American dream
The one that resurrected through tradition,
but no one cares because
we've all got our own problems

Bachelors of Life

I'm not sure whether I am going or coming, whether I have
left or I am still here
I was never certain like most with their college degrees
mounted high on their walls and their caps and gowns
tucked away in the back of their closets
I have lost sleep, but none because of caffeine dependency
I find myself yearning to stand still
Although I am tormented by my inner desire to retain facts
so I can boast and say I have learned many things
To achieve awards that prove I haven't just occupied space
But even those who are
are still not aware
That no one sees the world like you do

Disconnected

I heard my mother's voice
It sounded like glass
I heard my mother's voice
Shards found their way into my mouth
cutting my tongue
I heard my mother's voice
Begging for me to chew faster
I heard my mother's voice
Unpleasant
Unyielding

Bonus Tracks

Earth

My soul doesn't get caught up in what lives matter
Nor does it take polls in political banter
It only desires comfort from rain and earth
Warmth via contact
Simplicity from understanding not to get attached
And poetry that will exceed my physical lifespan

Origins

Keep it up
Life is tough
Don't give up
No money
Make do when the rents due
Only few understand what it means to be this hue
Ever wondered why the sky is black by night?
Only stars are in sight?
Dirt is brown
They fell asleep in darkness
Photos from their story developed in our dark room
Without us they wouldn't be here

Blinded

I want you to carry me
So these words don't get lost inside my dream
Tuck me into your bosom
And when the merchants ask for money pay them with the
pieces of paper damped with sweat from your cleavage
Tell the vendors to keep the loose change

Hieroglyph

I named him August and his twin the fourteenth
I knew twenty-sixteen would be different
So I let him leave seeds inside of me
It was toe-curling magic
I couldn't wait to see it all
In the hospital they all sat in the waiting room
I opened my legs and a bundle of words were
Born
I cried as I nursed commas, haikus, and lines
They were all mine
Reassuring me to love them so I took my time

Motherland

Swallow my mind I'm coming with thought
She said
Evolution suckled on her breasts that reared humanity
Somewhere along the way we hitchhiked from
Community and settled like colonists

Jamaica

My beloved smiles swaying her broad hips to reggae and
Calypso
Sipping red stripe slowly for 54 years is the secret to her
relaxed nature
There's rhythm and ease in everything she does
Outsiders privatizing soil that bares fruit for the locals
Leaving so many starving with pride
She's still beautiful

Woman you know how to confine me to the abyss of your
cursed womb
You bitter thorn
your scorn cold never be the reason I hold my head down
and let them use me
Untamed and unashamed
I'm burning the stories you told me as a child leaving
ashes behind as I rise like a phoenix

Not an ounce of compassion would unclench the umbilical
cord from around my neck
Choked as the air thinned
Pondering about my demise in the last few breaths
I remained calm and quietly grinned
It angered her to see that I stopped fighting what I
couldn't change
Her desire to keep holding on dwindled
I knew she wanted to prevail
But I rejected it
Nothing contained my rebellious spirit

Have you ever felt to the point of numbness?
Blood constricts and expands in my fingertips
Frozen glaciers hang like popsicles on the vessels of my
atrium

Betrayal is a funny thing even funnier when accompanied
by a laughing friend
The garden is healthy
And the grass
Stood six feet tall
No one saw it coming

I wanted to be angry, but I've starved that part of me
Pity lied
Laying on the foundations of a broken home,
Broken stones,
Broken bones
Please don't call me on
This broken phone

Her lips were sealed with two parts his saliva and one part
his breath against hers
Tonight a recipe for love
In 40 weeks a cradle of joy and laughter

I remember falling in love with potential
I waited for characteristics that dwelled in my imagination
to show up
I sacrificed
I struggled
I held on to my expectations
I resented him for not fitting the mold I placed him in
He was an ice cube
Our love melted
I wanted to believe we were on our way to bliss
Two years and seven months passed by
I stopped waiting for him to be the man in my dreams

Sounds of night echoes in my head
Night air resides under the tiny hairs on my bare arms
Gently tugging
short sleeves to come over and keep them warm

A tribute to the darkest hues

Dark chocolate is highly fortified
Some don't possess the enzymes to break it down, but
queens do
We'll digest you and rebuild nations
upon cacao fields

Hey love hey love
As you sit on the porch with the aroma of the sun on your
skin
I'm thawing out
Purple and blue chakras lure me in

I'm closing the other doors so I can finally open up to you.

He left every part of my being pulsating
My lips
Third eye
The worlds between my thighs
I was satisfied

I'm falling apart
I've grown to understand that's seasonal
Becoming leaves
Leaving shit behind
That I no longer need

This love thing ain't a spectator sport
You can stand on the sidelines and plot how you're going
to make your plays, but
When that Jones come to recruit you
You will get muddy
Eventually
You'll get scratched
And
Bloody

Sometimes I love deep
Sometimes I may want a little more than your right hand
on my thigh
But right now
I'm emotionally unavailable

Don't want your love
Don't want your pain
Don't want to sacrifice anything
Don't tell me about your day
Just want you to sit down and have dinner

The last time we kissed
I bit your lips
Then I captured your soul
And used it as notebook paper

The Composition

The Love Story Part I

Every Saturday she went inside the stationary store to pick
out items for her new apartment
She loved the scent of fresh paper
and often admired the old type writer that sat on a table by
the checkout counter
This place was
a writer's refuge

Love Story Part II

You again, he said smiling as she approached the counter
at the stationary store
Before she could pull out her wallet
he signaled for her to stop
I got this one
he insisted

Love Story Part III

She wondered why
Searching for lust in his bright pupils
She saw a friendly soul
Comfort
Warmth

Love Story Part IV

So tell me something, he said packing pens, loose lined
paper, and four journals of assorted sizes
What do you do?
I write, I make jewelry, and I'm a healer, she said
He held on to his grin

Love Story Part V

And you? She said
I work for myself
This is my store
I also have a studio in the downtown area of Barbados

Love Story Part VI

I didn't question or dispute the offer
I thanked him
he handed me a brown bag
I grabbed the handle and headed out the door

Later that day I began writing
The thought of his smile lingered on my mind
I turned blew out the flame in the lamp and went to sleep

Love Story Part VII

It was Saturday morning
I needed to go to the market and buy fruits, vegetables,
and fresh fish
I showered outdoors, brushed my teeth with clay
Went back inside rubbed shea butter onto my skin and
massaged olive oil onto my mane
Last, I grabbed a white cotton fabric a few yards long
draped, pinned and tucked it around myself
Put on the brown leather sandals by the back door
Walked outside towards the shed
Unlatched the door
Pushed my teal scooter out as I locked up
Rode out of the yard

Love Story Part VIII

Felt a warm touch on my shoulders
Startled
I looked to my right
It was him
About 6 feet tall
He wore torn denim overalls
Splattered with paint and a white t-shirt that clung to his
arms
His dreads were loose and hung close his waist
He smiled, saying hello

Love Story Part IX

I nodded to acknowledge him
I was in mid-sentence
Asking the elder woman how much per pound the
jackfruit and tamarind was
She looked at him
Hello Taj how yuh madda and them doin'
She doin' real good
I pickin' up some tings for her
She smiled
He found his way behind her stall and hugged her
She kissed him on the cheek
Gi harr my love when yuh si harr
He laughed
I will aunty Campbell, he said

Love Story Part X

Again he insisted on buying the items
Before I could say anything he handed a wad of cash to the
woman and thanked her
She counted and stretched her hand to give him change
He said that that's for you to keep
Mrs. Campbell and I both smiled and said thank you

He walked with me
We laughed
talked
I ought to go now I said as we approached the scooter.
I invited him to come for lunch in a park by my house
He agreed

At 3'clock he pulled into the park
I sat on the bench while the sweet smells
of curry shrimp enticed my taste buds
Sweet songs of Sade's "Soldier of love "serenades us in the
background
He brought potted gardenias,
mint infused lemonade
a blanket
two wine glasses
a hand crafted wooden stand
and a Nikon camera
We sat together and feasted on the spread
Listening to the sounds of nature
He smelled like cocoa butter

Outro

For my sister

The air is polluted between us
I've inhaled disloyalty
Where we stand isn't firm
Back at ground zero
If I've got to put on a dust mask
Just to visit you
It's best I love you from a distance

When it rains it pours so heavily
Instantly bringing back old memories
When it snows I feel you next to me
Summer time arrives and you're not here
Though I feel your presence near
These are the seasons of love

See there is something about you that keeps my lips from moving the way you talk so smooth and how you got me grooving

Excoriation

I've been picking
Hours have passed and a new sheath appears on my skin
I rip it off
And start again
The pain sent a rush to my brain
I know the scars are disfiguring and ugly
No backless dresses
One summer I only wore pants
Piled on the concealer onto my face
Dabbed foundation on my legs to conceal the shame
before I left my house
I wanted to stop picking
All I did was blame myself for tarnishing my beauty

I remember when loving you was the most challenging
task
I would ask friends and family to look after you because I
couldn't be bothered
You were too much to care for
Too much time
Too much energy
Too hard to look at
Awkwardly standing there
With your long arms and legs
Skinny little thing
I ignored you
But you tugged at my heartstrings for years
Begged me to love you
Sent me beautiful messages in the clouds
Still showed up to events and gatherings even though I
didn't want you there
Till one day I walked by a store front
Looked inside the window
It was you
Glowing and beautiful
Collar bones deep enough to fill with spring water from
that river
The same one we splashed and played in as children
Where I first discovered your reflection

You're not like them
The other women never wanted my mind they only
wanted my head
But you
You're different
I can tell
When I began to unzip my pants you told me to unravel
my thoughts instead

Pitiful
Where I was when I wanted it all
Bare
The scent of desperation misted on my wrist
Rub them together the stench lingered in the room
Compromised
Face facing the pillow
Back arched
Spread across the floor and torn
Discarded like unwanted junk mail

The only man I ever loved
Stains ink on my tongue
12 times a day
Penetrates my mind 5 days a week
The kind of love making that destresses and relaxes me
When I need therapy I straddle him Indian style
And wait
For more ink to drip
As I open my eyes to the words on my pages

Like Flo I'm all about progressives
Honey blood dripped from black hives
I'm your tour guide
Welcome to my life keep all your valuables inside
Enjoy the ride
Swallow my pill
Light sage and chill
The fumes are here to thrill
Those with closed minds inhale and become ill

I write for the little girl whose womb was tarnished by
inferiority
For the women who never knew happiness
And for the mothers whose mothers
Never taught them how to love themselves

Letting my pen bleed out the pain I feel
I've been feeding these pages
So I'm not filled
belly busting with regret
healing sorrow with words that used to torment
Patiently watching myself grow into a better me

There is something profound in the way one expresses
their truth
Poetry is pure expansion
No fear
Guilt
Or
Shame

Many thanks and much love to all who supported me during this process. You know who you are.

Xoxo,
Gissel

Social Media:

Instagram: gissel_grizzle

For Bookings, Questions, Comments and Concerns:

Email: loosesheets@gmail.com

To: Ros

Thank you for
your support.

With love

signature

♡